Clogpots
in Space

Scoular Anderson

A & C Black · London

First published 1994 by A & C Black (Publishers) Ltd
35 Bedford Row, London WC1R 4JH

Text and illustrations copyright © 1994 Scoular Anderson

ISBN 0–7136–3842–7

A CIP catalogue record for this book
is available from the British Library.

Filmset by Kalligraphic Design Ltd, Horley, Surrey
Printed in Great Britain by William Clowes Ltd, Beccles and London

Dexter Clogpot and his big brother Bernie were watching a horror film on TV . . .

It was about two space-travellers stranded on the planet Snirv.

One of the space travellers was about to be eaten by horrible green slimy Snirvians when suddenly . . .

. . . weird hands slithered round Bernie's neck.

It was Dexter's and Bernie's sister, Rosabella.

Hi, boys!

Come and see what I've bought!

She had just come back from the local jumble sale.

They all trooped outside.

Rosabella opened up the back of
their van . . .

. . . and pulled out . . .

A really big basket!

And a huge roll
of lovely red and
green cloth!

Rosabella could see the boys were
disappointed.

CHAPTER 2

The Clogpots weren't very brainy.
But they could work things out
slowly, and Bernie's brain had
started to tick.

First, they got Dexter to blow into it.

They tried Rosabella's hair-drier.

Then, Dexter went off to the hire-shop and came back with the proper machine for blowing up hot-air balloons.

At first the balloon wriggled.

Then it twitched.

Then it began to grow . . .

and grow . . .

and grow . . .

and grow . . .

Until . . .

Dexter
caught hold
of Blinko
just before
the basket
left the ground.

Then up they floated.

CHAPTER 3

To begin with, it was quite exciting. They had a good view of their town, Muddyflatts . . .

. . . and the countryside . . .

. . . and the sea.

Then they floated into a cloud.

Bernie looked around. He had never driven a balloon before.

But by now the sun was setting and it was getting dark.

The Clogpots were so tired after their exciting day that they fell asleep.

Dexter woke first.
It was very cold
and dark.

For a moment he wondered why the
rest of the family was curled up
beside him. Then he remembered.

He peered over the side of the
basket . . .

. . . and saw an
amazing sight.

He woke Rosabella and Bernie.

When all the Clogpots were awake
they stared out of the basket.

Rosabella was in no mood for excuses.

Bernie thought.

Then something nearby caught
his eye.

Bernie found an
extra piece of rope
lying in the
bottom of the
basket.

He made it
into a lasso.

Then he threw it . . .

. . . several times . . .

. . . until he caught the satellite.

33

Dexter began to climb across. The rope swung and sagged.

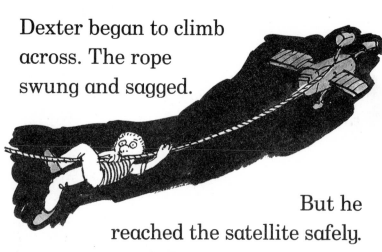

But he reached the satellite safely.

As he jumped for joy the satellite gave a creak and began to move away from the basket.

In a few seconds, Dexter and his satellite had disappeared into the blackness of outer space.

Rosabella was furious again.

And Rosabella sat down for a really good cry.

CHAPTER 5

Meanwhile, back in Muddyflatts, Mr Plummer was opening up his planetarium for the day.

He was feeling pleased with himself. The planetarium had just been repainted and Mr Plummer had installed a new control panel.

CAFÉ

ICES

SHOWS
AT
.15 PM
and
15 PM
DAILY

PLUMMER'S PLANETARIUM
special lighting
and sound effects
now installed

Experience a
life-like and
educational voyage
round the solar
system!

He was tidying up the litter round the door.

My new show should draw the crowds in thousands!

When he noticed a large piece of red and green material hanging down the wall.

Some people will leave their rubbish anywhere!

Mr Plummer was so short-sighted, he didn't notice that the piece of material was hanging from a ventilator shaft on the roof.

There were one or two other things that Mr Plummer didn't know that afternoon.

He didn't know that the Clogpots' hot-air balloon had fallen down his ventilator shaft.

He didn't know that Mrs Todpole
was stealing money from the cash
box and hiding it away.

He didn't know that Mr Smarmly
made faces behind his back.

He didn't know that the dentist was Mr Smarmly's cousin.

Mr Plummer didn't know just how exciting it was going to be.

CHAPTER 6

As soon as Mr Plummer had gone, Mr Smarmly puffed out his puny chest,

I'm in charge now!

and bossed Mrs Todpole around.

Remember we're letting the public in at 2 pm exactly.

I *know* that.

TICKETS

Stuck-up stick insect!

Mr Smarmly crept upstairs. He wasn't allowed in the control room,

but today he could sneak in and have a look.

He sat in Mr Plummer's seat and spread his hands over the control panel.

He imagined himself bringing up the lights on the planet Saturn. The audience would go "OOOH!' He imagined talking into the microphone.

He got up, walked into the planetarium and gazed up at the planets hanging in the dimness. Then a shiver ran down his spine. He could hear strange noises.

Mr Smarmly strained his ears. Yes, he could hear strange sounds . . .

MUNCH
MUNCH
MUNCH

Rosabella had
found a bar of chocolate in her bag.
She and Bernie were munching it,
sitting in the bottom of the basket
while they decided what to do.

. . . sounds he had never heard
before in the planetarium.
Really creepy sounds.

GROAN!

Dexter had fallen
off his satellite.

Just as Mr Smarmly was about to
turn on all the lights, Mrs Todpole
called him.

Oh, Mr
Smarmleeeee!

She was selling tickets.

Of course he hadn't returned, he was still with Mr Smarmly's cousin, the dentist.

CHAPTER 7

People were taking their seats in the planetarium.

Mr Smarmly went into the control room.

In a few moments he would raise
the curtains.

He would press buttons and flick
switches. Planets and stars would
move about on unseen wires and
pulleys.

Mr Smarmly switched on the lights
and turned up the music.
The show had begun.

On the TV monitor, Mr Smarmly noticed that something wasn't right.

He told himself it was just his imagination.

Mr Smarmly tried to calm himself,

but he could hear the audience
laughing. Things were going
very wrong.

Mr Smarmly dashed out of the control room to see what was happening . . .

. . . just as Dexter crept in.

There had been lots of noise. He had heard music and laughter. One minute it was dark, then lights went on and off again. He had fallen from a great height. Now he was confused.

Dexter began to press buttons and flick switches.

While Dexter
was trying to
work out how to
fly a spacecraft . . .

. . . Mr Smarmly
was trying to get
along a corridor . . .

. . . filled with
bits and pieces
left by the
workmen . . .

. . . when they
were doing up the
planetarium.

Then Dexter heard loud cheers.

I must have landed...

...on a strange planet, by the look of things.

He decided to go out.

I hope they're friendly.

I'll take this money as a gift.

Mr Plummer had arrived just as the performance was starting. He had never seen anything quite like it.

Earlier in the day there were lots of things that Mr Plummer didn't know. Now he knew . . .

. . . about Mr Smarmly

and Mrs Todpole . . .

. . . and the Clogpots.
The way the Clogpots had found
themselves in outer-space was the
funniest thing he had ever heard.

He gave Mr Smarmly and
Mrs Todpole the sack. But he
kept the Clogpots.

I have a brilliant idea! How would you like a job?

'Well,' said Rosabella . . .

'. . . who would have thought a visit to the jumble sale would end up like this!'